WHY THIS IS AN EASY READER

- This story has been carefully written to keep the young reader's interest high.
- It is told in a simple, open style, with a strong rhythm that adds enjoyment both to reading aloud and silent reading.
- There is a very high percentage of words repeated. It is this skillful repetition which helps the child to read independently. Seeing words again and again, he "practices" the vocabulary he knows, and learns with ease the words that are new.
- Only 125 words have been used, with plurals and root words counted once.

  Nearly one-half of the words in this story have been used at least three times.

  Some words have been used 15, 19, and 22 times.

ABOUT THIS STORY

- Another very satisfying story about the irresistible dog-hero, Barney Beagle. Cat lovers will like it, too! Like the other Barney Easy Readers, this one is a good way to meet first person story-telling. It is also a "natural" for encouraging even the shyest children to participate in discussion —about animals and people and relationships. Most youngsters will understand Barney's jealousy very well!

Barney Beagle and the Cat

Story *by* JEAN BETHELL
Pictures *by* RUTH WOOD
Editorial Consultant: LILIAN MOORE

Wonder® Books
ALLAN PUBLISHERS, INC.
Exclusive Distributors

Introduction

These books are meant to help the young reader discover what a delightful experience reading can be. The stories are such fun that they urge the child to try his new reading skills. They are so easy to read that they will encourage and strengthen him as a reader.

The adult will notice that the sentences aren't too long, the words aren't too hard, and the skillful repetition is like a helping hand. What the child will feel is: "This is a good story—and I can read it myself!"

For some children, the best way to meet these stories may be to hear them read aloud at first. Others, who are better prepared to read on their own, may need a little help in the beginning—help that is best given freely. Youngsters who have more experience in reading alone—whether in first or second or third grade—will have the immediate joy of reading "all by myself."

These books have been planned to help all young readers grow—in their pleasure in books and in their power to read them.

Lilian Moore
Specialist in Reading
Formerly of Division of Instructional Research,
New York City Board of Education

1981 PRINTING
Cover Copyright © 1981 GROSSET & DUNLAP, INC.
Copyright © 1965 by Wonder® Books, Inc.
All rights reserved under International and Pan-American Copyright Conventions.
Published simultaneously in Canada. Printed in the United States of America.
Published by GROSSET & DUNLAP, INC.
Exclusively distributed by Allan Publishers, Inc.
Wonder® Books is a trademark of GROSSET & DUNLAP, INC.
ISBN: 0-8241-5947-0

Hello.

I'm Barney Beagle.

This is where I live.

I like it here.

See this?

It's my bed.

Here's my dish.

And look at all my toys!

I have lots of fun.

I'm a lucky dog!

Here comes Alan.

Alan is my boy, you know.

I think every dog needs a
boy, don't you?

Alan needs me, too.

I'm his best friend.

What's that, Alan?

What is it?

17

Is it a dog?

No, Alan. You don't need two dogs.

I'M your dog.

Me, Barney Beagle!

But what is that?

What can it be?

Oh, my! It's a CAT!

20

Hello, Cat.

Ow! Stop that!

Alan! I don't like this cat.

Take her away!

Go away, Cat!

That's MY dish!

Stop that!

That's MY toy!

No! No!

That's MY bed!

Stop!

Give me that!

Alan, please!

Take this cat away.

You don't need her.

You have ME.

I'm your dog.

You're my boy!

Look at me, Alan. Look.

It's ME—Barney Beagle!

Oh, dear, he sent me away!

Alan sent me away!

He doesn't like me.

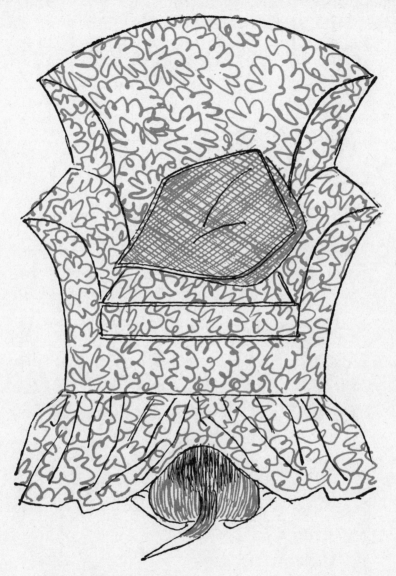

He likes that cat.

I wish that cat would go away!

There she is now.

Where is she going?

There she goes, out the door.

Stay out, Cat.

There she goes, down the street.

Keep going, Cat.

There she goes,
to the milk truck.

Now she's in the milk truck.

Oh, my! The man does not see her!

Oh! Oh! The man has shut the door!

There goes the truck.

Good-by, Cat!

Keep going, Cat!

No more Cat.

I'm glad.

Now Alan will be MY boy again.

Here he comes now.

What does he want?

Oh! He's looking for the cat.

I know where she is.

But I won't tell.

Alan looks and looks and looks.

He can't find her.

Oh, how sad he is!

Don't be sad, Alan.

Play with ME.

I can be funny.

See?

But Alan is still sad.

He wants the cat.

Alan is my boy.

I don't want him to be sad.

I'll tell him where she is.

Come on, Alan.

I'll take you to the cat.

This way, Alan.

Come with me.

Come on, Alan. This way.

The truck, the truck!

She's in the truck!

Let's run.

Run, Alan!

We must get to the truck on time!

Stop! Stop!

Stop the truck!

Come on, Alan.

Open the door.

There she is!

There's the cat!

Alan is so happy.

The cat is happy, too.

They do not need me, now.

Hey! What are you doing, Alan?

Look! Alan likes me!

Hey! What are YOU doing, Cat?

Look! The cat likes me, too!

Now I have TWO friends.

I told you—

I'm a lucky dog!